"Karen, did you say something just now?" Jonathan asked.

"She didn't, but I did," another answered inside his mind.

Jonathan clapped both hands to his head. Suddenly the skunk jumped on his lap and, planting both front paws firmly on his chest, looked him in the face.

"It's me, Tsynq Yr, operative of the Sylon Confederacy."

Jonathan's voice was on the high edge of hysteria. "Karen, are you some sort of weird ventriloquist?"

To her surprise, Karen suddenly felt sorry for him.

"Hey, Stinker, don't come on so strong," she said aloud. "You're a little hard to take all at once, you know."

"Sorry," the skunk thought in reply as he settled more sedately into Jonathan's lap. "Explain as you see fit."

STINKER FROM SPACE

Pamela F. Service

FAWCETT JUNIPER • NEW YORK

RLI: $\dfrac{\text{VL 6 \& up}}{\text{IL 7 \& up}}$

A Fawcett Juniper Book
Published by Ballantine Books
Copyright © 1988 by Pamela F. Service

Library of Congress Catalog Card Number: 87-25266

ISBN 0-449-70330-4

This edition published by arrangement with Charles Scribner's Sons, A Division of the Scribner Book Companies, Inc.

Manufactured in the United States of America

First Ballantine Books Edition: May 1989

For Doug

� contents ✖

▦ one ▦

FUGITIVE

AGAIN THE DEADLY BLUE LIGHT ENGULFED HIM. FLINCHing from the brilliance, Tsynq Yr struggled with the controls. Abruptly his scout ship veered away, and the cool glow faded.

He knew he was a crack space pilot, one of the best in the Sylon Confederacy, but that Zarnk cruiser was closing on him fast. He was hopelessly outgunned and outpowered in this cheap scout ship he'd had to steal to escape the orbital fort. What he wouldn't give now for his own trim little Sylon fighter.

Blue radiance flared again, and Tsynq Yr abruptly changed the ship's course. He could not let them get him now. Three years of miserable skulking and spying, and finally he'd pieced it all together. He'd found out the Zarnk plan for attacking the Delta Arm of the

1

Confederacy. He must get that information back to Sylon High Command, and he wasn't about to let a blundering Zarnk cruiser stop him.

The cramped cabin burst into blue glare. On Tsynq Yr's right, the control panel fizzed and crackled.

He surveyed the damage. Now that's done it! The stabilizers were out. There was only one choice left, he realized, and he didn't like it. The maneuver was difficult and dangerous at the best of times. In this piece of flying space scrap. . . .

Before the Zarnk could fire again, Tsynq Yr slid the drive control to the top of the scale, well beyond the safety limit. The little ship shuddered and shot off through space. With the rising speed, the blackness around him began to waver and vibrate as he neared the fringes of hyperspace. This ship was not equipped to make the jump into that dimension, but with skillful piloting and split-second timing, it skipped along the dimensional boundaries like a stone skips over water.

Tensely Tsynq Yr played the controls. If he didn't obliterate himself, this little trick should throw off pursuit for a time, enough time perhaps for him to repair the ship or find some Sylon reinforcements.

As space pulsed and shivered around the speeding ship, an alarming hum rose from the controls. That last Zarnk hit must have done more damage than he'd thought. Suddenly the hum turned into a scream and the ship abruptly lost speed, spinning off through black, star-spotted space.

When, with much cursing, he'd brought the spinning

under control, Tsynq Yr looked out at those stars. Where was he? Skipping along the edges of hyperspace played havoc with physical location, and he had no idea where he'd been dropped off. Of course, his pursuers wouldn't either, but that would be no help if he'd been plunked somewhere in the Zarnk Dominion.

But no, the stars showed he was in neither Zarnk nor Sylon territory. Terrific! Exploring uncharted regions was all very well, but not when he had top secret information to pass on.

A quick glance at the smoking control panel showed that here he was and here he was likely to remain, at least until he could work some repairs. He trained his scanners on the nearest star system. Planets, yes, mostly useless. One marginal, one fully habitable. He homed in on the latter.

If the Zarnk ever managed to trace his wild route here, this planet would be an all too obvious refuge, but he had no choice. His little ship was making new alarming sounds.

He sped toward the target, a globe swirling with greens and blues and whites. Pleasant-looking, all right, but too much water. With half the ship's systems out, this landing was going to be rough enough. Tsynq Yr hoped it would at least be on land.

Plummeting down toward the planet's night side, he knifed into the atmosphere. Too steep. He tried to pull up but failed. Worse, he seemed to be heading into a local storm system.

Dark clouds closed in. Everywhere the atmosphere

discharged in long forked bolts. Suddenly the ground, splotched with vegetation, was hurtling toward him. Too fast. Much too fast.

When Tsynq Yr awoke, he realized two things. First, his ship was nearly destroyed. Second, he was dying.

This body had served him well. At first, he'd taken it on merely as a convenience to his spy mission. Like most active Sylons, he'd lost track of how many bodies he'd used since the one he'd had at birth. But this body had worked well, was attractive in its own way—and he'd grown attached to it.

And he would die in it, too, if he didn't find a suitable host—soon. His mind cast about, seeking life forms. Vegetation was plentiful, but all seemed rooted and subintelligent. He sensed other creatures that did move, but he probed and found they weren't much more intelligent than the plants. Tiny flying creatures seemed interested only in finding out if his own dying body was good to eat.

Desperate now, he probed elsewhere. Here was something larger. It wriggled through the soil, but its brain was negligible. He doubted his intelligence could even fit into it. And besides, it had no appendages. He could never repair a ship in that body.

Suddenly the thing he probed at was snatched up and eaten by another creature. This new one would have to do. He hadn't the strength to look further. Yes, there was a brain, not a big one, but he'd worked with worse. And there were even hands of sorts.

With his last shred of strength, Tsynq Yr shot his being into the alien creature. The native's intelligence registered brief surprise before it was pushed to the back of the mind and the Sylon took over.

Beady black eyes blinked as he gazed at the alien world around him. Vegetation everywhere, tall and short, orange, brown, and green. Moisture blew from a clouded night sky. His eyes, it seemed, were designed for seeing in the near dark.

Curiously Tsynq Yr examined his new body. There was a head and a tail, and four short legs supporting a body that was low to the ground. Mammalian, apparently; the whole body was covered with hair.

That hair was clearly the most impressive feature. It was long, soft, and marked in a striking pattern. The background was glossy black. White capped the head, and two bold white stripes swept down the back and out onto the bushy plume of a tail. Quite handsome, really.

Meeting in the Woods

❖ two ❖

MEETING
IN THE WOODS

DARK DESTROYER DROPPED IN BESIDE THE PRINCESS OF Light. One by one the other action figures followed before Karen slammed down the lid.

Swinging the old battered lunchbox in one hand, she clattered down the stairs and into the kitchen. Her mother looked up, her face taut with the unfamiliar strain of sewing curtains.

"Going out to play?"

"Yes," Karen replied as she scooped several peanut butter cookies into her pocket.

Mrs. Blake's frustration over the curtains ricocheted against her daughter. "Karen, honestly! Why don't you ever play *with* anyone?"

"Oh, Mother! There's no one here I want to play with."

"We've been here two whole months now, Karen. Surely you've made some friends by now."

Karen swayed by the doorway, hand itching to grab the knob. "Oh sure, some of the girls at school are okay, but they aren't like. . . . They don't play my sort of games." She'd barely avoided saying "like Rachel." Her mother had threatened to scream if she whined any more about leaving her best friend behind in their old hometown.

Karen sidled toward the door. "These girls just want to dress up, put on makeup, and play with dolls."

"And those things in the lunchbox aren't dolls, I suppose?"

Karen sputtered indignantly. "These are action figures! They aren't silly dolls that wet and poop on demand. They're characters in great interstellar dramas, adventurers bounded only by imagination!"

She placed her hand on the doorknob and threw out a line that was sure to divert her mother's train of thought. "Besides, all the other girls live in town."

"Yes, your father *would* choose a picturesque 'handyman's delight' way out in the sticks." Mrs. Blake sighed and gave the curtain an angry stab with her needle. "But still, it's not completely isolated out here. Why don't you play with that kid who lives up the road?"

"But he's a boy!"

"Well, I can't help that. Besides, if you're so nuts about space, you two should be made for each other. I understand he's wacky over space, too."

7

"Mother, it's not the same at all. When Jonathan Waldron looks at stars, all he sees is numbers and facts—not the drama, the romance!"

Sewing calmly again, her mother seemed to ignore this comment. "I was talking with his mother the other day, and she said Jonathan's room is full of space posters and models, and he knows the names of every astronaut, Soviet or American, since the year dot."

"There weren't any astronauts in the year dot."

"Talk about being too factual! Oh, go on out and play."

Quickly Karen slipped out the door. Last night's storm had polished the sky to a bright blue. Against it, the autumn colors of the woods ahead rose like a jeweled crown.

Freed from parental plans, she skipped toward those trees, heading for the hidden clearing she had already made her special place. But as she hopped over the rain puddles, she found herself still thinking about Jonathan Waldron.

He might be interested in space, but he was a real nerd nonetheless. All numbers and no soul. It was bad enough having to ride the bus with him. But be friends with him? In school Jonathan was a whiz in math and science, but hopeless in English. His poems stank. Of course, she thought with a giggle, boys stink generally. Still, she wouldn't mind seeing his room and all those models and posters.

Reaching the clearing, Karen dropped all unpleasant thoughts. It was breathtakingly beautiful here. In the brilliant sunlight, the flaming red maple leaves glowed like stained glass. Settling down among the maple's gnarled roots, she leaned back and looked up at the gleaming leaves. She was a medieval princess taking refuge in an ancient cathedral. The stark white branches of the sycamore across the clearing were the soaring marble pillars. Or maybe she was a princess on another planet, taking refuge in the heart of the giant Sacred Jewel to escape the soldiers of the Dark Empire.

Opening the lunchbox, she spilled the action figures over the grass. Birds chirped busily in the leafy recesses of the woods. From a distance, the crisp air carried the tang of burning leaves. It mingled with the rich moldy odor of damp earth and fleeting whiffs of woodsy animals.

Although Tsynq Yr's first hours on this planet had been trying ones, he was fairly pleased with his new body. The creature's native intelligence was not high, but the brain was adaptable, and Sylon intelligence was very compact. And besides looking elegant, the little beast had some very interesting senses. Hearing and eyesight were keen, and there was another sense, the olfactory one, that he'd seldom had before. Life was suddenly full of interesting odors, not the least of which was his own.

The state of his ship, however, was far less satisfactory. It had smashed into the boggy earth, and the outside structure had all but disintegrated. Already the remains were sinking from sight. Somehow, he'd have to construct or borrow another vehicle.

That meant finding out something about the level of native civilization. During his fateful descent, the little ship's scanners had shown signs of civilization on this planet, but he had no idea how advanced it was.

He had set out to discover this about the time dawn came to this world, with its medium-size sun appearing in the east. His host's body was suddenly telling him it was time to sleep. He put aside that message easily enough, but messages from the empty stomach were harder to ignore.

His rations were gone with the ship, so he let his body's instincts take him to food. Soon he was industriously turning over dead logs and snapping up the bugs and fat white grubs underneath. He didn't dare let his own instincts rise to the surface, for fear he'd be instantly sick. Even so, the rotten raw bird's egg he ate was almost too much.

It was the smell of food enticing to both his selves that brought him to the clearing. Under a red-leafed tree, a bipedal creature was sitting, eating a round flat piece of food.

His mind as well as his sense of smell reached out, and instantly he realized that here was a species of considerable intelligence. Perhaps one of this planet's civilized beings. Artificial garments, large brain capacity. He probed into the thoughts.

There was a running account of soldiers of a vast interstellar empire pursuing the female monarch of a rival power. So these beings had achieved space travel. He was in luck!

He decided to make himself known—mentally. His new body clearly didn't have much speech ability. How should he start—ask what sort of space drive they used? Maybe he should inquire if they had any knowledge of the Sylon Confederacy or the Zarnk Dominion. Or maybe, part of him urged, he should just ask what the creature was eating.

"I am dreadfully hungry," he thought. "Would you share some of that?"

The girl looked startled, then muttered, "Karen, you dope, don't have Dark Destroyer ask for a peanut butter cookie."

"He wasn't asking, I was," came the thought as Tsynq Yr stepped into the clearing.

Karen's look of surprise changed to alarm. Slowly she stood up and began backing away.

The Sylon stopped advancing and studied her. She was clearly frightened—of him. Puzzled, he probed her mind. It had something to do with the olfactory sense. A word jumped to the front of her thoughts, a word with very negative associations. Skunk.

❈ three ❈

AN ALLIANCE

KAREN BACKED UP SLOWLY. SHE DIDN'T LIKE ABANDON-
ing her loyal band of action figures but was afraid any
sudden move would startle the skunk into stinking at
her.

"I won't stink at you!" came an indignant thought.

"You will, too. You're a skunk!" Karen shook her
head violently. "Hold it, kid," she said to herself.
"Better go play dress up with the other girls if you're
going to start making up dialogue for skunks."

"You didn't make it up. I said that. But don't worry
about your model creatures. My main interest at the
moment is with the object you're eating."

Bewildered, Karen looked at the half-eaten peanut
butter cookie in her hand. Hesitantly she threw it into
the clearing. "Here," she said aloud. "But if you think

I'm going to talk, or think, at animals that can't talk, you're crazy.''

Tsynq Yr waddled toward the cookie and after an ecstatic sniff began munching, his thoughts unhindered by the crumbs in his mouth. "Delicious. But you are being most unreasonable. I am obviously not an animal that can't talk, since you are talking with me.''

"You *are* an animal that can't talk!'' she thought back. "You are a skunk, and skunks can't talk.''

"Obviously, then, I am not a skunk. This is really very good. Have you got any more?''

Automatically her hand went to her pocket and she threw another cookie onto the grass. "So what are you then? You certainly look like a skunk. And smell like one, too, I bet.'' Suddenly she clenched her fists. "No! I will not talk, or *think*, at a skunk!'' Deliberately she turned around and started walking away.

"Oh well, I suppose you aren't intelligent enough for curiosity.''

"Don't you think insults at me!''

"You were thinking some pretty insulting things about my odor.''

"That's because you're a . . . Oh, this is impossible! All right, all right, what are you if you are *not* a skunk? And don't think I believe in you just because I'm thinking at you.'' She took a few steps back. The black and white creature in front of her was licking crumbs off the grass.

"First let me ask you if the terms Zarnk or Sylon are familiar to you.''

"No, they're not." Mentally the answer felt honest to him. "But," she continued, "I asked you a question first."

"All right, then, I'll tell you. I'm in the Space Corps of the Sylon Confederacy. A Zarnk cruiser was after me, and I had to oscillate along the hyperspace boundary to escape. My flimsy little scout ship was damaged, however, and I spun out into this sector. Then when I tried to land here for repairs the ship was completely wrecked. Now I need help getting off your planet."

"Oh," Karen said, sitting down again at the base of the tree. Her mind registered fear, fading into doubt, fading into interest and finally excitement. But there was no extreme surprise, confirming for Tsynq Yr that these people were familiar with space travel and extra-planetary life.

"So," Karen said aloud, leaning back against the tree trunk, "let me get this straight. You're a skunk from outer space, some bad guys are after you, and you need to get back to some place out there." She waved a hand vaguely at the leaf framed sky.

"Right. Except I am not really a skunk. I borrowed this body from a passerby. My earlier body was fatally injured in the crash."

"Wow," she said shaking her head. "Do you change bodies all the time?"

"No, not all the time. It takes too much energy. I only do it in dire need."

"Oh." She was silent a moment, then reached into her pocket. "Would you like another?"

"Yes indeed. What are they?" He ambled forward, his white striped nose twitching eagerly.

"They're cookies, made with peanut butter."

"Peanut butter?" His whiskers tickled her outstretched hand as, squatting on his hind legs, he retrieved another cookie. "I imagine I'd like this in any body. Maybe I should take some home with me."

Karen sat back and looked at the fat furry creature. Skunks were really kind of cute if you didn't worry about the stink. "So, how do you plan to get back if your ship's wrecked?"

"I was hoping you could help me with that."

"Me? I don't know anything about spaceships. I'm just a kid."

"An immature member of the species? Ah. Well, perhaps you could direct me to the nearest spaceport."

"Spaceport? We haven't any."

"No? But I thought . . . Well, maybe what I should do first is learn a little about your civilization. You are certain, now, that you know nothing of the Zarnk Dominion?"

"Zarnk Dominion? No, never heard of it. Is it anything like the Dark Empire?"

He scanned her mind for the reference. "Yes, somewhat similar."

"Ah, real nasties. Well then, I guess I'll have to help you escape." She frowned thoughtfully for a minute. "If you want to learn more about Earth, maybe you could come home with me and read the encyclopedia. That has stuff about everything I've ever had to do a school paper on."

"Yes, perhaps that would be the wisest course. Do you perhaps . . . uh, have any more peanut butter cookies at this home of yours?"

"Sure. Peanut butter cookies, and I think there are still some peanut butter–dip granola bars. And there's a jar of peanut butter, and some straight peanuts too if there are any left from my parents' party last week."

Mentally he sighed with contentment. "This body of mine seems to be constantly hungry."

Karen stood up and walked across the leaf-strewn clearing. Eagerly the skunk followed. In a few minutes they had emerged from the trees and started along a faint footpath in the weedy meadow. In the brilliant autumn sunlight, the skunk's black and white stood out boldly against the yellowed grass.

Karen turned and looked at her bizarre new companion. "Have you a name?" Deliberately she thought the question. This form of communication would take getting used to.

"Yes, I am called Tsynq Yr."

"Stinker?" She whooped with laughter. "Your name is Stinker?"

"No, no. Not pronounced like that. Tsynq Yr."

But she was laughing too hard to detect any difference. "Oh, that's perfect. Perfect!"

The Sylon thought he should probably be insulted, but if it amused this alien so much to mangle his name, he supposed it was acceptable. Particularly if she provided more of that peanut butter.

four

"CAN WE KEEP HIM?"

AS KAREN APPROACHED THE OLD WHITE FARMHOUSE, IT occurred to her that Stinker might not be a totally welcome guest. She decided to go around to the front door and make a direct dash for the hall stairs, hoping her mother was still struggling with curtains in the kitchen.

Leading the waddling skunk, she walked stealthily around the house to the front porch and quietly opened the door. Her mother was standing in the hall, a stricken look on her face.

"Karen," she whispered hoarsely, "I saw it from the window but was afraid to shout. Do you know there's a . . . a skunk following you?"

"Oh. Yes. His name is Stinker. He's . . . uh, someone's pet, I think. He's very tame."

"How do you know? Oh dear, he's coming in! Get him out of here before he sprays!"

"Really, he's very friendly, so he must be a pet. And I'm sure he's deodorized." She shot a thought at Stinker: "If you make a stink now, I'll skin you."

"Oh, but a skunk, Karen! Maybe he's rabid. That could be why he's not acting like a wild skunk." Her voice had a panicky edge.

"No, no, he must be somebody's pet. Look, he does tricks." She reached down and grabbed their dog's battered tennis ball from the floor, then bounced it along the hall. "Fetch!" she said pointedly.

Stinker got the picture.

Feeling like an idiot, he ambled after the ball, chasing it as it ricocheted off the umbrella stand. Eventually he threw himself on top of the thing. Then, managing to get his jaws around it, he carried it awkwardly back to Karen and laid it at her feet.

"There, you see?" she said pleadingly.

"Well. . . ."

Just then, Stinker heard toenails click on the floorboards behind him. He spun around and was gripped by an almost uncontrollable urge to lift his tail at the golden-haired creature behind him. But he caught a mental wave of horror from Karen and concentrated instead on trying to communicate with the thing.

"I'm a friend," he told it. "I belong here. I like you."

The spaniel whined and wagged his stump of a tail. Slowly it walked up and began smelling the skunk.

"We can have nice times together," Stinker continued at the dog. "We can play together, chase the ball, find loathsome things to eat."

The dog sat down in front of the newcomer and grinned amiably.

Karen's mother watched with amazement. "Well, will you look at that? I've never seen Sancho act like that with a strange animal. He's usually all stiff legs and growls."

"See? Stinker must be a pet. Perfectly safe and odorless. Can we keep him?"

"Well . . . I suppose we'll have to keep him until we can find the owner." She stood for a moment looking thoughtfully at the skunk. "You know, he is kind of cute at that."

Stinker cringed at the word but decided he had better play up to it. This person was obviously an authority figure. Sitting on his broad hind end, he wrapped his tail around him and tucked his two forepaws under his chin.

"Don't overdo it," Karen thought at him.

Her mother's expression was quavering between a smile and a worried frown. "Oh dear, I don't know what to do. I guess your father could drop an ad by the newspaper office tomorrow on his way to work. But maybe we should just take the skunk to the animal shelter."

"Oh, no!"

"Well . . . maybe not yet. But that's just until someone's had a chance to answer the ad. And, Karen, you have to take him on walks frequently. I hope he's housebroken.''

"Oh, I'm sure he is," Karen said, adding the thought that he'd darn well better be.

"And it'll be your job to feed him. I wonder what skunks eat."

"Peanut butter," Karen answered without thinking.

"How do you know?"

"Oh, I read it someplace."

"Well, whatever. But taking care of him will be your responsibility entirely until we can see if someone answers the ad. Understand?"

"Yes, Mother. No problem. Let's go upstairs, Stinker."

As they trotted up the carpeted stairs, Stinker thought, "I presume there is some reason for not revealing my identity to your mother?"

"Sure. She's an adult."

"So?"

"Adults don't believe weird things very easily."

Once in Karen's room, her guest set about a thorough exploration. Drawers and boxes were opened and plowed through, the tape recorder was put through its paces, the pencil sharpener was twirled and then taken apart. All the while, Karen picked up little mental bursts of surprise, interest, amusement, and occasional disdain. She also realized that apparently a space explorer's training did not include putting things back as you found them. She hated to think what her mother would say if she came in now.

"Uh, Stinker, if you want to see the encyclopedia, it's over here. It's just a junior edition, of course, but . . . say, can you read?"

Stinker gave the mental equivalent of an indignant snort. "Of course. I picked that up out of your mind."

Karen raised startled hands to her head. That sneaky skunk's worse than a pickpocket, she thought.

Stinker looked up from the jewelbox he was examining, a plastic bangle dangling over one ear. "Sorry. Don't mean to offend you. I forget you're not used to working with your mind this way."

"Oh, that's okay. Take what you need, I guess. At least it doesn't hurt. I'll go down and fix us some peanut butter sandwiches."

When she returned with a plate of sandwiches and a couple of oranges, Karen found the skunk squatted in front of volume A of the encyclopedia, smoothly scanning a page, then turning it with his little furry paws.

She stopped in the doorway and stared. This more than anything else convinced her of Stinker's story. After all, talking animals were old hat—in fairy tales, at least. But *reading* animals . . .

She stepped into the room, quickly closing the door behind her. "Don't let my folks catch you doing that—or typing or turning on the TV. Take your cue from Sancho. He's probably about as stupid as your average skunk."

"Sancho? Is that what that type of animal is called?"

"No, he's a dog. Sancho's his name. They called

him that because when I was little I couldn't say 'cocker spaniel.' It came out 'cockeyed Spaniard.' ''

"Oh." He didn't get the allusion, and from a scan of Karen's mind, he could tell she wasn't too clear about it either. Something to do with a character in some large boring book.

The next day, when it was time for school, Karen left Stinker in her room with a bowl of peanuts, the last of the peanut butter cookies and several apples—the apples being an attempt at balancing his diet.

Before leaving to catch the bus, she took his picture with her father's Polaroid camera. She had wanted to take Stinker along in person to show the kids at school, but her parents had firmly said no. It would probably cause a riot, they thought, and Karen decided that fun as that might be, they were probably right. But at least she could flaunt the picture. Having an apparently pet skunk seemed to Karen a surefire way to raise her prestige at this new school.

On the bus coming home, Jonathan Waldron actually sat next to her and after a few awkward minutes asked to see the picture. He seemed genuinely impressed. Smugly Karen thought how impressed Jonathan would be if he knew the truth about this particular skunk. Let him keep his old spaceship models!

Back in her room again, Karen found Stinker just finishing volume U. The floor was littered with peanut shells and apple cores, and Sancho was flopped on a rug, soulful brown eyes fixed lovingly on his new friend.

She plunked down a stack of books onto her bed. "I

took out some books on space travel from the school library. That encyclopedia's not very up to date for scientific stuff."

"Oh, glad to hear it," Stinker thought back at her. "I was beginning to wonder—though I've been learning a lot about the ancient city of Ur and also Ulysses and Ungulates." He got up, shook himself, and began waddling toward the bed.

"Not yet," she said firmly, placing a hand on the pile of books. "All work and no play makes a dull skunk, also maybe a dead one."

"Huh? But I don't want to play. My dignity. . . ."

"Never mind your dignity! As far as anyone can tell, you are a skunk. Dad took that ad to the paper this morning. In a few days, maybe a week, when nobody claims you, they'll want to take you to the pound—unless you've proven what a fine family pet you make."

Stinker picked up her mental image of the animal pound. "Right." He turned to Sancho. "Let's go play."

✖ five ✖

DESPAIR OF A
STRANDED SKUNK

WHEN KAREN'S FATHER GOT OUT OF HIS CAR THAT NIGHT, he was greeted by the sight of his daughter playing ball with a cocker spaniel and a skunk. He watched with amazement as the little black and white player continuously outwitted the flop-eared golden one.

"That's some animal," he said, shaking his head in grudging admiration, as he walked up to Karen. "I never would have guessed a skunk could make such a good pet. He's really quite bright. His owner ought to be eager to get him back. Just don't let him go wandering off, Karen. We don't want him bringing back any of his woodsy friends."

"Oh, don't worry, Dad. Stinker's a real home lover." As her father walked away, Karen continued to herself, "It's just that his home's some distance away."

When she turned back to the animals, she found Stinker and Sancho sitting side by side, vigorously scratching themselves with hind feet. The dog seemed resigned to it, but his companion was not.

"I don't think much of these little biting creatures that seem to have come with this body," Stinker thought at Karen. "I keep giving them mental commands to leave. They do, but they have apallingly short memories."

"I don't think fleas are known for their high intelligence," Karen replied. "Just don't scratch much in front of Mom and Dad. They'd make you wear a flea collar. Then you'd smell worse than a . . ."

"Do stop making uncomplimentary references to odor."

Stinker also did not think much of the dog kibbles Karen's mother served him for dinner, although on the kitchen floor beside him, Sancho eagerly gobbled up his own bowlful. The skunk forced some down, however, after Karen sprinkled them with peanut butter morsels.

After dinner, he took a quick look at the new space flight books, then settled down in Karen's lap in the living room while the family watched a movie on television. It was a popular space saga with plenty of interstellar dogfights and blazing lasers. Stinker watched with excited intensity.

Karen's father noticed, "Look at that skunk, will you?" he laughed. "You'd almost think he was following the story."

"Oh, no," Karen protested quickly. "I'm sure he just likes the moving shapes, or maybe it's the food

25

commercials.'' She felt an annoyed kick from a hairy paw.

After the movie when Stinker and Karen had gone upstairs, he shot a question at her. "How old are those books you brought back, anyway?"

"The space flight ones? Oh, pretty old, I guess. Ten years, maybe."

"Only that old? Then how could you people have moved in a few years from the primitive stuff in the books to what we were watching tonight?"

"Oh, that was just a story. It's made up."

"A story! But . . . what about all that other stuff you know about? The Dark Destroyer, the Princess of Light?"

"They're just stories, too. But, heck, if I hadn't been into that sort of thing I'd probably never have believed *you* so easily."

His mental groan went to Karen's heart. Suddenly understanding, she knelt down beside him. "You mean, you thought . . ."

His bushy tail drooped. "I mean, this might not have been the best planet to crash land on."

When Karen came home from school the next day, she found Stinker pacing back and forth across her room. "It's hopeless!" he thought at her. "These books make it clear. I'd have as good a chance of getting home from here if I sprouted wings and tried to fly."

She sat down and scooped the dejected animal into her lap. With one hand she scratched the white patch on his head, while the other traced the pattern along his back. Despite himself Stinker purred, rubbing against her fingers.

"You know," she said, "you're welcome to stay here if my parents say it's okay."

"Thanks," he answered dully. "I mean, I appreciate the sentiment, but I simply can't stay here. Sylon High Command must receive the information I have about the Zarnk attack."

After a moment the skunk got up from Karen's lap, ruffled his long silky fur, and with determination padded toward the door. "I guess I should go back and take another look at that wreck. Maybe there is something I can do with it after all."

Soon, with Sancho trotting eagerly behind, they slipped out the back door and headed off to the woods.

In his former body, Stinker realized, he'd probably have had trouble finding the crash site again, but this one led them right to it. The land here was so boggy that already the landing scar and even the wreckage of the ship were disappearing under mud and watery green scum.

He felt slightly squeamish about confronting the remains of his former body—he had been very attached to it—but he found that the forest scavengers had rather thoroughly removed all traces. Indignantly, he wished indigestion on them. He did not care for the thought of having been somebody's dinner, not at any stage.

Karen sat on a fallen log and watched as Stinker scrambled over the remains of his ship, digging here and there, Sancho enthusiastically helping.

From what Karen could see sticking above the surface, this might almost be another old rusted car that had been dumped in the woods. For an interstellar adventurer, she decided, this fellow seemed awfully low profile: a peanut-guzzling skunk who arrived in a broken-down jalopy. Oh well, maybe he cuts a more impressive figure in his own setting.

He looked far from impressive when he finally came back to the log, bedraggled and covered with mud. He crawled up beside Karen, his tail drooping dejectedly over the side. Irrepressibly cheerful, Sancho sat at Karen's feet, panting and thumping his short tail against the ground.

Stinker sighed. "It seems the drive unit is pretty well intact, but the ship itself is a total write-off. Those mass-produced scout ships ought to be banned from the market. At home I have a trim little one-person fighter that could have taken a landing like that with hardly a scratch." He sighed again and began picking absently at the rotten bark. Without thinking, he popped a grub into his mouth.

"Well, if the engine still runs," Karen said, trying to ignore the grub, "maybe you could build a new ship."

"With the technology you have on this backward rock? Ha! You might as well ask those ancient people of Ur to build an automobile."

Karen bristled at the slur to her planet but had to admit, after some reflection, that he was probably right. "It's getting late," she said, standing up. "We'd better head back. You may have see-in-the-dark eyes, but I haven't.''

The woods were cold and purpling with coming night when the three stepped from their shadows. High above, the last rays of sun were lighting a vapor trail as it etched a white line across the deep blue sky.

"What about putting your engine in an airplane?" Karen suggested suddenly.

"Too flimsy," came the dejected reply. "Even the best wouldn't last more than a few minutes outside the atmosphere."

As they approached home, Stinker's head hung low and his muddy tail dragged listlessly along the ground. Karen had never seen an animal look so depressed.

"Hey, you'd better perk up, or my mother will want to take you to the vet."

Stinker got a mental picture of shots and pills and having thermometers stuck up his hind-end—and quickly his head and tail rose jauntily into the air.

As they walked in the front door, they could hear the drone of television. Picking up Stinker, she settled onto the couch beside her father's recliner. The evening news was on with its usual display of maps, film clips, and serious, neatly groomed announcers.

Sitting listlessly in Karen's lap, Stinker paid little attention until suddenly his little ears swiveled around like radar. On the screen an announcer talked about a space shuttle flight to take place in two weeks. Stinker's beady black eyes sparkled, and he squirmed about in Karen's lap.

Her father looked over. "Has that creature got fleas?"

"Oh, no. It's . . . it's just that skunks in the wild are nocturnal animals. He still gets kind of antsy at sunset." Karen had been reading the encyclopedia too. With the excited skunk tucked awkwardly under one arm, Karen stood up, "Guess I'll go wash for dinner."

"Can't you hold still?" she thought at Stinker when she'd reached the top of the stairs.

"Well, put me down then. I've got feet! Why wasn't that ship written up in those space books?"

"Oh, I guess it was only in the planning stages when they were written. But why? All it does is orbit a few times and land again."

"But it was designed for space travel! Where it goes depends on the propulsion system—and the pilot."

"Maybe, but . . . Hey, what do you have in mind, anyway?"

"It's obvious. We have to hijack the space shuttle."

✖ six ✖

AN ALLIANCE
EXPANDED

QUICKLY KAREN SHUT HER BEDROOM DOOR BEHIND THEM.
"You're crazy! They launch those things down in Florida, behind lots of fences, with lots of guards around.
They're not about to let some skunk march up and take over the ship."

Stinker sat down, resting his chin on crossed paws.
"Hmm, that *does* pose difficulties—the security arrangements, I mean. Obviously we'll have to bring it down somewhere close, where there's no one to guard it."

"*What?*"

"Those flat fields up the road should do."

"You want to make the space shuttle land in the Waldrons' soybean fields?"

"Yes, that would be fine. Then we wouldn't have to drag my drive unit very far."

"I don't like the way you keep thinking 'we.' "

Stinker's whiskers drooped and his black eyes looked pathetic. "But of course I'll need your help, I don't know very much about this space shuttle of yours."

"It isn't mine! It belongs to a bunch of scientists. And anyway, I don't know the first thing about it. I'm not like nerdy Jonathan."

"Oh. Who is this Jonathan? A friend of yours?"

"Not a friend! No . . . an acquaintance."

"Well then, let's go ask him about the shuttle."

"I can't!"

"Why not? Does he live very far from here?"

"No, he lives just up the road. But I can't go up there and talk with him."

"Why not?"

"He's a boy!"

Stinker was silent a moment. "I was not aware that males of your species were mute. Your father certainly is not."

"No, no, it's just that . . . Oh, all right, all right. We'll go talk with him. But I wouldn't do this for just any skunk!"

With one excuse or another, Karen managed to put off the ordeal until Saturday, but at last she could delay no longer.

The day was gray and overcast, like her mood. After breakfast, she trudged up the road with Stinker trotting jauntily behind. As they approached the large gray farmhouse, Karen felt it looked more like a forbidding medieval fortress or some wizard's lair in an alternate universe.

With heavy hand, she knocked on the front door, desperately hoping the entire family was out, but to her despair, a woman opened the door and smiled inquiringly.

"Good morning, Mrs. Waldron. Uh . . . the other day Jonathan said he was interested in seeing my pet skunk, and . . . and so I've brought him over."

"Oh . . . yes." The smile wavered and Mrs. Waldron took an involuntary step back.

"Oh, don't worry. He's deodorized and very friendly."

"Yes. Yes, certainly. Jonathan did talk about him. I'm sure he'll be delighted. I'll go tell him you're here." Hastily she disappeared from the doorway, leaving Karen to stand brooding on the porch.

Stinker thought at her, "I don't understand, Karen. If this person is your age, your neighbor, and your schoolmate, why aren't you friends?"

She groaned. "Social customs far too complex for you to understand."

From upstairs came the sound of Jonathan's mother knocking on a door, and then a muffled "Yes?"

Blushing guiltily, Karen took a step inside to hear better. "Karen from down the road is here to see you, Jonathan."

"What? She's a girl! Tell her I'm sick or something."

"I know she's a girl, silly. It wouldn't kill you to talk

with one. Besides, she's brought that pet skunk you were going on about.''

Silence. Then, ''Well, all right. Send her up.''

''Yes, your lordship. 'Send her up,' indeed.''

Hastily Karen stepped back, but she felt better. She had something Jonathan wanted. And it seemed he didn't like to be with girls any more than she did with boys. Well, they'd just have to endure each other for the sake of the universe.

Keeping a cautious distance, Mrs. Waldron ushered Karen and Stinker up the stairs and through the door.

As she stepped into the room, Karen looked around curiously. Hanging by transparent threads from the ceiling was a fleet of plastic spacecraft. Not all were Russian or American models. There were a fair sprinkling of Klingon and Romulan battle cruisers, Imperial fighters and other fantastic craft. Walls not lined with bookshelves were covered with posters. Prosaic sky charts and NASA publicity posters mixed with cinemagraphic heroes and villains brandishing weapons. On one table sat Jonathan's ham radio set she'd heard about, and on the other was the terminal for a home computer.

Then her eyes fell on Jonathan, who sat slumped down behind a desk strewn with pieces of a half-finished model of a space fighter. Sunlight from the window glinted off his glasses. ''Well?'' he said coldly.

He sounds just like Ming the Merciless giving audience, Karen thought. ''Uh . . . hello, Jonathan. I sort of thought you'd like to meet my pet skunk.''

On cue, Stinker waddled out from behind her and began exploring the room. With nothing to say to each other, Karen and Jonathan concentrated on watching the skunk.

Bookcases were examined, drawers opened, and the radio given thorough scrutiny. When Stinker's inquisitive paws began twirling a black globe dotted with pin-sized holes, Karen couldn't help asking, "What's that?"

"That," said Jonathan in a grand tone, "is my planetarium. I'll show you." Now honestly eager, he jumped up, pulled down the window shades, and flipped a switch on the base of the globe. Suddenly the darkened room was transformed into a starry sky. Tiny pinpricks of light shone on the walls and ceiling in rough semblance of constellations.

"See, there's Orion and Taurus and the Pleiades." He went on to point out the other constellations, distorted somewhat as they bent around corners or splayed over furniture. Finally opening the shades, he sat down again. "Pretty neat, huh?"

"Primitive but effective," came an answer. "A little too schematic and two-dimensional to be useful for navigation, though."

"Well, of course. . . ." Jonathan stopped awkwardly. "Karen, did you say something just now?"

"She didn't, but I did," another answered inside his mind.

Jonathan clapped both hands to his head. Suddenly

the skunk jumped on his lap and, planting both front paws firmly on his chest, looked him in the face.

"It's me, Tsynq Yr, operative of the Sylon Confederacy."

Jonathan's voice was on the high edge of hysteria. "Karen, are you some sort of weird ventriloquist?"

To her surprise, Karen suddenly felt sorry for him. "Hey, Stinker, don't come on so strong," she said aloud. "You're a little hard to take all at once, you know."

"Sorry," the skunk thought in reply as he settled more sedately into Jonathan's lap. "Explain as you see fit."

Karen did, with Stinker throwing in an occasional supplementary thought. Afterwards, Jonathan looked across at Karen, trying to avoid seeing the skunk who was now on his desk busily assembling pieces of his model.

"And I'm supposed to believe that?"

Karen got up from the edge of the table where she'd been sitting. "Well, isn't it better than believing in a mind-melding skunk who could probably beat you in computer games?"

He looked down at the busy little black paws. "Yes, I guess it is." He was silent a minute. "But what I really can't believe is that I'd be of any use in trying to hijack the space shuttle. I mean, that's really crazy!"

"Ah, but what I need first is information," Stinker thought at him as he slotted the plastic space pilot into the cockpit. "I need to learn everything I can about the shuttle's design and operation. Engine plans, reentry procedures, that sort of thing."

Karen snorted, thinking it unlikely that her neighbor could supply anything of the sort. But Jonathan, regaining some of his composure, shot her a superior glare.

"Sure, I've got most of that. If a kid writes a sincere enough letter, the NASA public relations people'll send most anything."

Jonathan rummaged through drawers and shelves and stacks of papers until he had built a considerable pile of booklets and brochures on the floor by his desk. Stinker, who was having difficulties with the little tube of glue, happily abandoned the model and climbed down. He began spreading the material over the rug, turning pages, examining diagrams, occasionally emitting little squeals and grunts of satisfaction.

The other two watched in awkward silence until there came a sudden knock at the door. "Can I get you kids something to eat?" Mrs. Waldron's voice said. "It's lunchtime."

Jonathan jumped up and hurled himself against the door. He didn't care to explain the studiously reading skunk, should his mother come in. "Oh yeah, great idea, Mom. Thanks. How about some sandwiches?"

"Make them peanut butter," came an unvoiced addition. On the other side of the door, Mrs. Waldron shook her head and went down to make peanut butter sandwiches.

37

When the last sandwich had been eaten, Stinker began thinking at them excitedly while using his tail to wipe off the peanut butter he'd smeared over the cover of *The Child's First Book of the Space Shuttle*.

"I believe I can do it. Some more detailed plans would be useful, of course. These things are awfully schematic. But I do think it can be done. I'll need your help for the next stage, though."

"Wait a minute, Stinky. . . ."

"Tsynq Yr, if you please."

"All right, all right, Stinker. Showing you kiddies' books and NASA PR stuff is one thing. But I'm not sure I want to help you storm the launchpad, firing lasers or whatever, and take over the shuttle. I mean, they've got lots of soldiers and everything around there. And machine guns, I bet."

"Oh, well, I actually hadn't planned anything as adventurous as that. Are you disappointed?"

"Disappointed?" Karen said. "Hardly. It's just that . . . well, it's just that stealing valuable U.S. Government property for a pet skunk . . ."

"Pet skunk!" came the injured reply. "I thought we were friends. I mean, even if you two can't manage to be friends with each other, you can both be with me, can't you?"

"Oh sure, but . . ."

"So what are friends for? They're to help each other. Right?"

"Sure but . . ."

"So I'll help you both to have a small, relatively safe adventure, and you help me get off the planet. And don't worry about the U.S. Government. I can see that their property's returned when I'm through with it."

"Well. . . ."

Stinker jumped up and waddled toward the door. "Now the first thing I need to do is dig that power unit out of my ship before it sinks any farther into the ooze."

"Sure," Jonathan said resignedly as he reached for his jacket. "What are friends for?"

❖ s e v e n ❖

BADDIES AT ONE'S DOORSTEP

THEY STOPPED AT THE WALDRONS' BARN FOR A COUPLE of shovels, then continued down the road to Karen's house. In the dilapidated gardening shed they clattered about, moving rakes and hoes until they pulled free an old red wagon. After a moment's thought, Karen hurried to the kitchen door and stuck her head in.

"I'm off to play in the woods, Mom. Already had lunch."

Her mother peered through the window above the sink. "Oh, you have Jonathan with you. How nice."

Karen's stomach churned at the sight of her mother's pleased smile. She stalked away. The sacrifices one had to make for interstellar adventure!

Karen and Jonathan took turns hauling the wagon. It rattled and wobbled behind them as the three set out toward the woods. Some of the leaves had fallen in the previous day's rain and now lay in a sodden carpet underfoot. Other trees still blazed their leaves against the lead gray sky. Brave torches against the encroaching power of darkness, Karen thought, shivering. The woods didn't look nearly so friendly today.

Unerringly they made their way to the crash site. As forest mingled with bog, the air smelled of damp earth and rotting vegetation. Their wagon bumped noisily over roots and fallen branches. The silence they disturbed had a waiting menace about it.

At first Jonathan was disappointed with the ship itself, but as he poked and prodded among the exposed remains, he became more impressed. "This sure is weird-feeling metal."

"No-good cheap stuff," was Stinker's reply. "My own Sylon fighter would never have broken up like this."

"I don't understand why nobody saw the crash," Jonathan said as he fingered an odd fragment of machinery.

Karen answered. "It was really stormy that night, remember? What with all the lightning, a falling spaceship or two would never have been noticed."

With the children wielding shovels and Stinker alternately directing them and scrabbling with his paws, they slowly cleared away part of the wreck. After a while, among twisted metal shards, they began exposing a smooth metallic cylinder elaborated with numerous odd projections.

"Is that what we're looking for?" Jonathan said, pushing sweaty hair out from behind his glasses. "It looks in pretty good shape."

"Yes. These units, at least, are made to last—even when they're put in a piece of space junk like this ship."

Struggling and heaving, the three managed to drag the thing out of the ground and into the wagon. The wheels sank into the muck with wet sucking sounds until they finally hauled it onto stony ground. Then, damp with sweat and mud, they sat down wearily on a mossy hummock to catch their breath.

A few birds chirped halfheartedly in the gray woods. Otherwise the only sound was the dripping of foggy dampness from tree branches and a faint rattling, like wind-stirred reeds.

Suddenly Stinker stiffened, his fur bristling like a porcupine's. "Did you hear that?"

"What?" Jonathan said. "The birds, the wind?"

"That rattling. Hurry, we've got to get out of here!" The little animal scurried over to the wagon. "Come on! I can't pull this by myself."

Catching his fear, though not knowing why, Jonathan and Karen jumped up and joined him.

"But I don't get it," Karen said as she pushed the balky wagon while Jonathan pulled. "What's the hurry?" Slowly their charge creaked forward with its heavy load.

"That noise! It's them! They've found me."

"Who?"

The rattling noise was suddenly closer, sounding like wind chimes made from dried bones. Stinker's thoughts hissed like a snake. "The Zarnk!"

There was a sudden movement in the grayness to their left. Karen and Jonathan spun around to see something emerging from bushes twenty feet away. It looked like a loose collection of bamboo poles held together at the top by a huge glob of amber glue.

The thing clattered forward. It stopped and slowly raised one pole-like appendage. Something metallic glinted at its end.

"It's armed, run!" squeaked a mental order. And the two children ran. Stinker bolted after them, but after a few bounds he suddenly stopped and reared up on his hind legs.

Karen, seeing this out of the corner of her eye, gasped and skidded to a halt. "Oh, no! His skunk instincts are taking over!"

Stinker thrust his tail into the air, aimed at the advancing enemy, and sprayed. A cloud of oily stench shot toward the thing.

The creature continued forward. Suddenly it stopped, swayed, and shrieked like a bagpipe. The gelatinous mass at its top began to solidify and crack. Blindly the thing staggered back and forth, its top disintegrating into powdery shards. The shrieking died hollowly away, and the pole legs clattered to the ground.

"Wow!" Jonathan blurted out. His legs were suddenly trembling as they staggered back toward Stinker.

"I guess those Zarnk guys are allergic to skunk spray."

Karen was shivering, wishing she hadn't seen what she just had. That was nightmare material, for sure. She shook her head. "Some allergy! All I've ever had is a rash from eating shellfish."

Stinker was silent, his nose twitching as he gazed at his fallen enemy. "I can't believe it," he muttered mentally. "That Zarnk nearly shot me. I wanted to run, and this idiotic body made me do that instead. I've never seen that happen to a Zarnk before."

"First class chemical warfare," Jonathan said, trying to sound calm through chattering teeth.

"It certainly was," the skunk answered thoughtfully.

"Uh, Stinker," Karen ventured, "are there likely to be any more of those things about?"

"Huh? Oh, no, not likely. He was probably a lone scout sent to follow my trail. But we'd better get moving. If he got some sort of message off, they might investigate sooner or later."

With renewed commitment, they hauled the wagon out of the woods and aimed their procession toward Karen's house. "We can hide this thing in the gardening shed," she suggested. "My mom won't be pottering around in there again until spring."

After dragging the wagon into the cramped, musty-smelling shed, they stuffed it into a corner, then covered it with half-filled bags of mulch. For added effect, they stacked some rakes, hoes, and trellises against it.

Finally they stepped back out into the gray daylight, and Karen firmly shut the shed door.

She wished she could shut her mind as firmly against the memories of that thing in the woods. Here was space adventure at her doorstep, but somehow it wasn't as clean and exciting as maybe meeting the Dark Destroyer or the Princess of Light. It was downright scary.

eight

The Best Laid Plans . . .

During the next week, Karen and her skunk were regular afterschool visitors at Jonathan's house. Both mothers acted insufferably pleased, much to their children's annoyance. Theirs was, as Jonathan said pointedly, "purely a business relationship in support of a mutual friend."

Stinker soon turned from examining the shuttle information to tearing apart the ham radio. At first this put Jonathan in a dither, but the little skunk did seem to know what he was doing. When handling human-designed tools for a job proved too difficult, he'd use his sharp little claws.

"But I really don't understand," Jonathan had said early on, "how this is going to help. I mean, ham radios don't pick up NASA—not the secret important stuff, anyway."

"Ah yes, but it's wonderful what a little tinkering can do, particularly when I can link things up with your home computer here. It is incredibly primitive, but it does what we need, just the same."

"And exactly what do we need?" Karen asked.

"We need to change the reentry programming and bring the shuttle down in that field out there."

Karen looked out the window, pulling aside the curtains with their red and blue rocket-ship design. Jonathan followed her gaze, a frown wrinkling his forehead.

"I hate to be a spoilsport, but I don't think the shuttle can land on a soybean field. It's too uneven, too many ruts. The landing gear is pretty much like an ordinary airplane's, you know."

"You mean your airplanes can't land on a flat surface like that?"

"Well, there aren't any huge bumps, but it's hardly flat, not smooth anyway. That's why planes need paved runways or dry lakebeds or something, so they don't flip over while they're landing."

Stinker thought something that did not translate. Then he clambered up on the window sill and glowered out. "All right. Next assignment, team. I'll look up the width of the shuttle's axle, and you two go down and measure the width of that road."

"The road!" Karen exclaimed.

"Why not? It's straight for a long distance. Quite long enough, I think."

Jonathan looked at Karen, sighed, then went to his closet and fetched a yardstick that carried the legend

47

"Time Measures All Things," courtesy of a funeral home. Soon the two were headed outside.

The road never carried much traffic, so it wasn't long before they felt safe getting down on hands and knees and measuring the width of the pavement and the hard gravelly shoulder.

"This is crazy, you know," Jonathan muttered as he scuttled like a crab over the asphalt.

"Yeah, particularly since this whole thing is probably going to fail."

"Good thing, too."

Karen looked at him. "You mean you don't want him to succeed? Then why . . . ?"

"Oh, I *want* him to. That'd be best, sure. But have you thought about what happens to accomplices of folks who hijack space shuttles?"

She swallowed hard. "Well, no. No one's ever done it before."

"Then we may be the first to find out."

Steadily the date drew nearer for the proposed launch of the shuttle. Karen and her furry companion regularly watched the evening news for any references to it. Her father commented on her commendable new interest in public affairs, which she hastily attributed to her current events unit at school.

One night after the news, while the family was eating dinner, a large expensive-looking car rolled up their gravel drive. Through their dining room window they saw a middle-aged woman with a great beehive of hair get out of the car and walk importantly toward their door.

Karen's mother answered as soon as the doorbell rang, and the strange woman gushed in. "Hello, hello. I am Mrs. Van Voorhis. I should have phoned I know, but I couldn't wait. I wanted to come right away and surprise everyone."

"Uh . . . yes," Karen's mother said. "But about what?"

"It's your ad in the paper. I've come to retrieve my dear little Flower."

"Flower?"

"The skunk, my dear. You advertised that you found my pet skunk."

Karen suddenly jumped up from the table. "Oh, but Stinker can't be yours!"

"Stinker indeed!" Then she smiled. "But yes, he must be mine. I lost my little Flower while passing through your town last spring when we were driving back from Florida. My sister-in-law chanced upon your ad in the paper and sent it on to me. The skunk you found must be mine, dear. Tame skunks aren't very common, you know."

"Maybe not, but this one isn't yours."

"You can't be sure of that, Karen," her mother said. "He very well might be."

In the kitchen where Stinker had been eating with Sancho, he'd picked up Karen's alarm. Now he had pushed his way through the swinging door and was making like a furtive shadow along the wall toward the stairs.

But Mrs. Van Voorhis caught a glimpse of black and white. "Ah, there he is now, my sweet little Flower. Come to Mama, Sweetkins!"

Stinker darted for the open door. As the creature dashed between his legs, Karen's father reached down and grabbed him around the middle. Stinker squirmed and thrashed but was held firm. "Quick, Helen, get me something to put him in!"

Karen's mother looked around frantically. Running into the living room, she dumped out some books they'd been boxing for a rummage sale and hurried back with the box.

Squealing "No, no!" Karen tried to grab Stinker away, but her father managed to cram the squirming animal into the box and jam down the lid.

"Here," he said, handing the box to the woman, his lips a tight angry line. "It would have been better if you'd called first. We've all become rather attached to him, I'm afraid. But I'm sure Stink . . . Flower will be happy with his rightful owner again."

Awkwardly the woman took the box as it thumped and jumped from inside. "Yes, I understand. He's such a little sweetie pie, I can see how he'd win anyone's heart. And I am so grateful for you taking care of him all this time. Isn't there something I can . . ."

"No, no. I think you'd better just go now. Good-bye, Mrs. Van Voorhis."

The door closed and Karen burst into tears. "Oh, Daddy, how could you?"

"Karen," he said firmly. "I liked him, too. But he was her skunk. To keep him, once we knew that, would have been theft."

"But we *didn't* know that. Skunks do look a lot alike, but he wasn't her skunk!"

"He had to be. She was right: tame skunks are not very common. And she lost hers right around here. It'd be too much of a coincidence to have two skunks like him in the area."

Karen stared at her father. "Oh, you don't understand!" she wailed, then turned and ran up the stairs. She slammed her bedroom door behind her. No, she thought miserably, you won't find two skunks like that very easily. Not two stranded skunks from outer space.

❈ nine ❈

A MISSING CONSPIRATOR

KAREN FOUND THE NEXT FEW DAYS NEARLY UNBEARABLE.
For a while she thought that if Stinker could just get to a
phone, he'd call, and she and Jonathan could set up a
rescue. But then she realized that was silly. After all, he
couldn't talk, not out loud, and she imagined one couldn't
just think over a telephone.

Finally the day of the shuttle launch arrived. Earlier,
Karen had planned to play sick so she could stay home
from school and watch it. Now she couldn't wait to get
away from the house and the morning radio's chatter
about the upcoming launch.

Grimly she stood by the roadside in front of her
house waiting for the school bus. She looked up as
Jonathan plodded dejectedly down the road to join
her.

"No word, I take it," he said flatly.

"None."

"I don't get it. I mean, surely he could have gotten away from that woman by now. She wouldn't know she was dealing with more than your average skunk intelligence."

"Yeah, but in the meantime, she could have driven three states away. I don't guess it's very easy for unescorted skunks to travel long distances. He couldn't just hop a Greyhound."

They were silent a moment. Karen thought about skunks trudging along highways and about all the dead skunks you always see in the middle of roads. "And think of the dangers of traveling that far. Cars and dogs and . . ."

"And Zarnk."

"Oh, no!" she exclaimed. "You think there could be more of them?"

"Stinker said there was a chance that the one fellow could have gotten off a message. And later when he looked and couldn't find that Zarnk's ship, he said it could have been programmed to go into orbit after a certain time and act as a beacon."

Karen shivered at the thought of a Zarnk hit squad clattering about. She was actually relieved when the bus came and took them off to the comforting normality of school.

In the afternoon, the school bus dropped her off at home just as the mail truck was pulling away. Her mother was already out at the box sorting through the mail.

"Bills, ads, and bank statements. Dull, dull. Here's something for you, Karen. My word, it looks as if it's been dragged through the gutter. You'd think the postal service would take better care of things."

She handed Karen a pictureless prestamped postcard. It was creased down the middle and blotted with a coffee stain. On one side an address was written and just as neatly crossed out in ink, while beside it in stubby pencil her own name and address was written in a clumsy childish hand. Perplexed, she flipped the card over and scanned the penciled message. Her heart leaped.

"Karen: Escaped crazy lady. Have important errand. Will be back in time. Please lay in big stock of peanuts, peanut butter, etc. Your friend, S."

She whooped with delight and ran up the road to show Jonathan. She found him in his kitchen, putting together an afterschool snack.

He read the card and his normally solemn face bloomed into smiles. "Boy, it looks like he pulled this out of some garbage can. Must have rooted around for hours before he found something he could reuse. Guess he figured most post offices wouldn't sell stamps to a skunk."

"I wonder what his important errand is."

"I don't know, but he'd better come back soon. He's monkeyed with my radio so much, I'm afraid to touch it. I might disintegrate myself or something."

Karen was about to chide him for caring more about his old radio than their friend. But she stopped. Clearly Jonathan was very happy to hear that Stinker was all right.

"Well," she said after a minute, "at least we can get on the provisioning detail. Maybe instead of catching the bus after school we should go stock up at the grocery store and walk home."

Jonathan groaned at the thought of the long walk. "Yeah, I guess we'll have to. Can't exactly ask our mothers to pick up a crate of peanut butter next time they're at the store—not without a few questions. Do you suppose real skunks like the stuff as much as space skunks?"

"Probably. I think skunks like everything. But let's lay in some lettuce or something else too, so he doesn't get scurvy."

The next day they told their parents they'd be late getting home from school. It was nearly dusk when they finally staggered up the road from town, grocery bags bulging with peanuts, peanut butter, peanut butter cookies, and bags of dried apples. Allowance hoards had been severely depleted, and all the way back Jonathan had grumbled about the unlikelihood of getting repaid by the Sylon government.

At last, slipping into the gardening shed they hid the

provisions with the alien engine under bags of mulch and potting soil.

The next few days were passed in anxious waiting. Homework suffered, but neither Karen nor Jonathan missed a word that TV or radio had to say about the ongoing shuttle flight. They knew who was spacewalking outside the ship and testing what pieces of equipment. They knew the family background of every astronaut, which scientific tests were successful and which firmly refused to work, and they knew what the crew ate and who got most severely space sick.

Karen went to bed with technical terms buzzing around in her head: extravehicular activity, O-ring seals, solid fuel boosters, manned maneuvering units. She knew the shuttle was orbiting 185 miles up at a speed of some 17,270 miles per hour. She never used to have any interest in these details but now found them surprisingly compelling. Even the Princess of Light, she grudgingly admitted, had to know how her flittership worked when she set off on some space adventure.

As the days of the mission passed by with no sign of Stinker, Karen and Jonathan became worried again. One news item on a local station caught Karen's interest for a moment because it dealt with skunks. State police several counties to their north had reported an unusual migration of skunks, a black and white wave pouring across the highway like lemmings marching to the sea. The announcer treated it like a joke, quipping that they'd have to add Skunk Alert to other things like Tornado Warning and Winter Storm Watch.

It was interesting enough, but Karen didn't see how it could have anything to do with Stinker. She just hoped that farmers didn't get so upset at the thought of hordes of skunks that they'd shoot one on sight. As the days passed she kept worrying more and more about farmers with guns, and dogs, and cars, and . . . even Zarnk. It didn't help her sleep any.

The day before the shuttle was scheduled to land, Karen and Jonathan avoided each other on the bus and at school. Both of them almost believed that their adventure and possibly their friend had come to an end. But somehow it seemed that if they didn't speak these words it wouldn't be true. That night Karen ate very little and went to bed early, causing her mother to worry that she was ill.

She dreamed that Mr. Spock of the Starship Enterprise was teamed up with the Princess of Light, who looked remarkably like the teacher Karen had had back in second grade. Hiding on a garbage truck, they were trying to escape from samurai warriors whose main weapon seemed to be bamboo wind chimes that they shook threateningly. Mr. Spock, who, to nobody's apparent surprise, had sprouted a skunk tail, was trying to construct a grenade out of empty peanut butter jars, when suddenly one of the wind chimes came alive and started loping down the road after their slowly escaping garbage truck. The Princess of Light desperately hurled peanut shells at it.

Shivering and sweaty, Karen woke up. She could still

hear the clatter of peanut shells against bamboo. The sound outlasted the wisps of dream.

She sat up and stared fearfully at her window. Outside in the dark, one branch seemed to be bobbing up and down, tapping rhythmically against the glass pane. A dark lump squatted on the branch, and from it came the glint of eyes.

✽ ten ✽

UNSCHEDULED STOP

KAREN WAS AT THE WINDOW IN ONE LEAP. STRUGGLING with the latch, she slid up the lower half of the window. The dark lump moved awkwardly down the branch, almost falling onto the window sill.

A thought buzzed in her head. "Remember reading in the encyclopedia that skunks are not natural climbers? Let me tell you, they were right. Whew!" Stinker belly-flopped to the floor as his quivering little legs gave out totally.

Instantly, Karen scooped him into her lap and stroked his matted, brier-studded fur. "Oh, Stinker, I'm so glad to see you. We thought that dogs or Zarnk had got you."

"Zarnk? You haven't seen any of them, have you?"

"No, but I have an overactive imagination when it comes to disasters."

"Ah, yes. Well, there's no time for imagination or explanations now, I'm afraid. Skunk legs are maddeningly short; things took much longer than I'd planned. The shuttle will be breaking orbit soon. I've got to get to Jonathan's, and I need your help."

"Sure. What can I do?"

"Well, I can't just go knock on his door in the middle of the night. And there's no tree by his bedroom window—not that I would *ever* try that again. I was thinking of throwing something against his window so he'd come down and let me in. But skunks, I've discovered, have pretty poor aim."

"I can do that for you at least. Let me put on some clothes first, though. I don't have your lovely fur coat for prancing about in the cold. Oh, Stinker, I'm so glad you're safe!" She hugged the skunk and hurried to get dressed.

It took a number of pebbles against the window to wake their confederate. Karen thought that this sort of thing seemed to work a lot better in the movies. But finally Jonathan's tousled head appeared at the window. In the pale haze of moonlight, Karen pointed at Stinker and then at the door.

The head disappeared. In a minute there was a faint click and the kitchen door swung open. Karen and Stinker slipped in beside Jonathan, and the three scuttled up the stairs to his room.

Once the door was closed and the light switched on, Stinker took a brief look around the room. "Excellent, everything just as I left it. Now, I'd better get to work." He scrambled onto the table that carried the now modified ham radio and computer. "Uh, Jonathan, you wouldn't happen to have any peanut butter cookies about, would you? I've been eating nothing but grubs, worms, and people's garbage for days."

Jonathan rummaged around in a drawer. "How about Chocolate Peanut Nuggets?"

"Lovely."

As Stinker chewed, he thought at Karen, "Now, you'd better get back home, young lady. You don't want people to talk."

"Don't be rude!" she shot back. But she admitted, the last thing she wanted was to be caught in a boy's bedroom at night.

"What do you need me to do there?"

"Nothing. Just go back to bed. Get up at the regular time and get ready for school as usual."

"What! You expect me to go off to school and miss all the fun?"

"Hey no, calm down. I just want you to act like normal. Go out and wait for the bus with Jonathan. Trust me. I won't let you miss any adventure."

Still disgruntled, Karen slipped quietly out of the room and down the stairs. She let herself out of the house and sped like a shadow down the road to her own home. All right, she'd trust him. But he'd sure better not let her miss anything. And she certainly didn't know how that bossy skunk expected her to get any more sleep.

The alarm woke her. She lay in bed a moment,

surprised that she was already dressed. Then she remembered. Jumping up, she ran a brush through her hair and hurried downstairs.

"My, you're ready early," her mother said as she tended the bacon.

"Umm. Well, it's sort of a get-up-and-do kind of day."

Her father came in, and as part of the morning ritual switched on the radio. ". . . no explanation, but the NASA spokesman repeated that the shuttle reentry is not going as programmed. The orbital maneuvering engines fired at the wrong time. The shuttle remains in the correct reentry posture, but its present position may not allow it to land where planned. Attempts to abort the reentry apparently have failed. But NASA spokesmen stress that at present there is no danger to the crew."

Karen just sat and stared at the radio. Then guiltily she poured cereal into her bowl and began eating it, forgetting to pour on the milk.

"Those computers!" her father said as he poured his own cereal. "Once they get it in their heads to do something, there's no stopping them. I hope those hotshot scientists had the sense to put in some manual controls as well or the thing may land in Russia or the ocean."

"Oh my, let's hope not," her mother said as she served up the bacon. "Karen dear, don't you want any milk on your cereal?"

"Oh." Karen suddenly choked on the dry flakes. "No, it's . . . too fattening."

Her mother gave her a knowing smile. "Little miss, suddenly worried about her figure."

Normally Karen would have bristled at that remark. Now she barely noted it as she reached to turn up the radio. " . . .reports that all attempts at manual override have failed. The shuttle continues to stick to an unprogrammed flight plan. And now it seems that radio contact with the crew has been lost."

Somehow Karen got through breakfast. The radio news switched to other items, repeatedly coming back to the out-of-control shuttle. Only with the greatest reluctance did she finally don her backpack and trudge out to the road. Maybe she could hop off at the next busstop and run back.

Jonathan was already there looking tense and tired. When she came up he whispered, "After you left last night, Stinker had me move all that stuff from the shed and hide it in that clump of willows beside the road there. I wish he wasn't so concerned about your 'reputation.' I could have used some help."

"Yeah, I think his view of Earth customs is a little dated. I let him watch too many old movies on television."

They were silent a while. One car whizzed past them stirring up an eddy of dry leaves. Dawn was turning the sky into a huge shell of Easter-egg pink. From habit, they watched the long gray stretch of road. Finally they saw the distant blot of the approaching school bus.

"I don't know about you," Karen said quietly, "but I don't want to get on that bus."

"I know," Jonathan muttered. "Stinker said to trust him but, I mean . . ." Suddenly he broke off. In the sky above the school bus another blot could be seen. It glinted silver.

"Holy cow," he said. "Look at that! It's the shuttle!"

Karen stared entranced as the silver speck took shape: wings and a pointed beak like a great metallic bird. It hurtled toward them, lower and lower along the line of road. The distant bus came to a screeching halt as the driver noticed the competition directly overhead.

A window-shaking roar filled the sky. Both Karen's and Jonathan's parents ran out of their houses as the graceful spacecraft touched down, its landing wheels rolling neatly along the hard shoulder of the road.

Over the noise, two sets of parents called for their children to run, but fascinated by the sight, Karen and Jonathan stayed put. Hadn't their friend said to trust him? With a dying roar, the ship slowed to a halt on the stretch of road between the two farmhouses, right beside an innocent-looking clump of willows.

✵ eleven ✵

CHAOS ON THE FARM

FOR A LONG MOMENT, SILENCE HUNG HEAVILY IN THE AIR. Then the watchers began talking among themselves and slowly walking toward the huge out-of-place vehicle.

After several minutes, a metallic click came from the side of the ship, and the hatch slowly opened. Cautiously a man in a flight suit peered out.

"Uh, good morning. Madam, may I use your telephone?"

From then on the day progressed in steadily increasing pandemonium. With no rolling airport stairs on hand, Mr. Waldron had to fetch his ladder for the crew, all of whom were anxious to leave a ship that had apparently developed a mind of its own. Phone calls were made and hospitality for the astronauts was divided between the two houses. Soon police sirens were heard, followed shortly by the sounds of fire engines and ambulances. Even though their services weren't needed, their drivers couldn't pass up the excitement.

By mid-morning the army arrived and blocked off the road, though that had been effectively done already by the imposing bulk of the spacecraft itself. Shortly afterward, flustered officials from NASA landed in a flock of helicopters.

The number of television and radio crews was increasing by the hour. Their helicopters chopped and whirred through the air, circled for good camera shots, then settled into the fields. Soon they and the media that had arrived by road surrounded the two farmhouses like swarming insects.

Much earlier on, however, there had been no observers. The astronauts and their hosts had been inside making perplexed phone calls and eating toast and coffee. Had any glanced out a window, a clump of willows would have screened their view of two children and a skunk hauling an odd-looking metal cylinder up the ladder into the shuttle's open hatch.

"Are you sure you've got this all figured out?" Jonathan had grumbled, palming sweat from his forehead. "When they launch these things down in Florida they've got great huge booster rockets and tons of fuel—solid and liquid. How can this doohicky of yours replace all that?"

Karen had been wondering the same thing but had been afraid to sound like a scientific dummy by asking it.

The skunk couldn't contribute much muscle power to the effort but puffed and wheezed prodigiously as he pushed his furry shoulders against the metal. "It's not my fault your people's ideas of propulsion are back in the stone age." They hauled it up another rung. "This ship's designed fine for space flight—a little clumsy, but it'll do. All those rockets, though"—he grunted as they cleared one more rung—"hopelessly primitive."

"So what's in this tin can of yours?" Jonathan asked, giving it an annoyed heave.

"I bet it's matter/antimatter," Karen ventured. She might not be a science whiz, but she did watch "Star Trek."

"Close," the skunk admitted. "More of a contained dimensional overlap. Pure matter/antimatter reactions are too volatile."

With a final shove, they hoisted the alien engine through the hatch. "Whew!" Stinker gasped. "You know, I once used a body that could have lifted that thing like a pebble. I never could have fit it in this ship, though. Let's roll the unit over there, and I'll start hooking it up."

"Need any help with that part?" Jonathan asked hopefully.

"No, that's a piece of cake. Speaking of which . . ."

"Yeah, yeah, the peanuts," Karen said. "Let's haul up those grocery bags, Jonathan. Then we'd better get back. It'll look funny if we're not there, all agog over a house full of astronauts."

Shortly after the two children slipped back to their

homes, one of the astronauts thought to come out and close the hatch against possible curiosity seekers. He never noticed the small black and white mammal tinkering quietly in the shadowy cabin.

Once the military had arrived, the area was cordoned off. It was midafternoon when a NASA engineer climbed Mr. Waldron's ladder intending to check out the shuttle controls.

Watching from her porch, Karen held her breath as the young man pushed open the hatch and disappeared inside. A moment's silence was broken by a blood curdling shriek. The man burst through the hatch and scrambled down the ladder coughing and fanning a hand in front of his face. Following right behind him came a cloud of noxious odor and a streak of black and white that darted down the ladder, through the legs of startled soldiers, and off into the woods.

The soldiers backed away from the reeking engineer who between coughs said, "The crazy thing must've climbed in when the hatch was open. The place stinks. Won't be able to go in for hours. Do I need a shower!"

He ran up onto Karen's porch. Karen held the door open with one hand, covering her face with the other, more to hide her giggles than to escape his odor. Her mother, on the phone with a radio reporter, wrinkled her nose, pointed to the bathroom down the hall, then continued her conversation. "Well, we were just finishing breakfast. . . ."

Karen closed the door and, with Sancho at her heels, wandered out toward the road. She wondered what had become of the school bus. The driver, she knew, was a very unflappable type. When he'd seen that the road was being used as a runway, he'd probably just decided to turn around and skip their stop. She bet that the kids already on the bus had been hopping mad that he'd turned away from all the action.

But not many local people were missing it now. The army had sent in reinforcements to keep back the steadily growing crowd. There was a rumor afloat that terrorists had somehow forced down the shuttle, though why they chose this particular stretch of soybean fields and farmhouses was not explained. People in the crowd kept looking sideways at each other, checking to see if anyone looked like a terrorist.

Karen's and Jonathan's families were allowed to remain inside the cordoned off area. Karen wasn't sure if this was because they were under surveillance or because they went with the houses. She suspected the latter. There didn't seem to be much of a thought-out security plan in effect, but then, this was hardly the sort of event anyone would have planned for.

From where she was, Karen could see a number of schoolmates outside in the crowd. She realized that ought to make her feel smug and important and was annoyed that it didn't. Adventures, she decided, may seem fine from a distance, but when they were actually happening to you they were mainly worry—and fear.

A military man, covered with meaningful-looking bits of braid and medals, was talking importantly to a television crew in front of Jonathan's house. Karen wandered over.

"The removal of the craft at this point is awaiting the arrival of the special truck designed to carry it. That has to come halfway across the country from the intended landing site, so it will be hours yet." At a reporter's question, he snapped, "No, I repeat, we have no idea why it landed here. The crew is being flown back to the Cape now for debriefing. And, of course, the ship and its computer will be thoroughly examined once it has . . . uh, aired out."

Just outside the security barriers, an enterprising lady was selling donuts and coffee from the back of her van. She was doing a booming business. Karen slipped up to Jonathan who was methodically licking maple frosting off his fingers.

"Did you see that NASA guy leave the ship?" she asked in a whisper.

Jonathan laughed conspiratorially. "I sure did. He acted like the devil himself was after him."

"Skunks do seem to have that effect on people," she giggled. "But why did Stinker leave, too? I mean, now he'll just have to sneak back in again."

"He thought at me in passing," Jonathan replied. "Said he'd finished hooking up his power unit and was off to get the others."

"Others? What did he mean by that?"

"Don't know. But he'd better be back before NASA's special truck gets here."

Another hour passed. It was beginning to get dark.

The TV crews switched on their lights and flooded the stranded shuttle with unearthly white glare. Then the squeal of sirens was heard again on the road.

Karen and Jonathan hurried to see what was coming. State police cars were racing toward them, escorting a long, oddly arranged truck.

"That stupid skunk had better hurry," Jonathan yelled at her over the noise.

The TV crews moved in. The now haggard military man was explaining, "Yes, but it seems that the second truck with the loading equipment had a breakdown. It should be here shortly, though."

"Hurry up, Stinker!" Karen thought intensely, but she picked up no reply.

Retreating to her porch, she sat on a deck chair, then got up, went inside, and came back with a plaid blanket. The evening air was clear but carried a sharp autumn chill. Karen cocooned herself in the blanket and watched the bizarre scene around her. Despite her anxiety, her eyes kept closing. Last night's disturbed sleep was catching up with her.

Sounds and voices became illogically muddled. A warm, sleepy buzz wrapped around her. Distantly it was sliced into by exclamations. "Ooh, did you see that?" "Shooting stars!" "What a show we're getting tonight."

That's nice, Karen thought drowsily. Shooting stars. Meteors, dropping to earth like . . . like spaceships! Her eyes flew open. She leaped to the front of the porch just in time to see the last of the shooting stars. A piercing arch of light, it cut through the purpling sky and disappeared beyond some distant trees.

Oh please, she thought, let it be just shooting stars.

Running off the porch, she pushed her way through the milling crowd of officials. One of them was frowning over some special-looking radio that was squawking at him about radar blips. She finally found Jonathan at the edge of one of his father's fields looking over the huge shuttle transport truck. Just then someone in the crowd behind them screamed.

"Eeek! Look out, a skunk!"

✦ twelve ✦

THE ENEMY

KAREN AND JONATHAN SPUN AROUND TO SEE A STREAK of black and white shooting through the horrified crowd toward them. With its funny rippling run, it looked more like a huge caterpillar, but the thoughts Stinker shot at them were far from humorous.

"Come on, guys, I need help!"

"Zarnk?" Karen thought back fearfully.

"Yes, three ships. But I'll try to take care of them myself. I need your help with my recruits."

"Huh?"

"All those days, I was off recruiting more skunks. I figured Sylon High Command would find them and their spray very interesting. Last night, I told them all to wait in the clearing while I redid the engines. But the empty-heads scattered looking for grubs, and while I was rounding them up again the Zarnk landed. Now I've got to try to sabotage their ships so they don't interfere with our escape. So I need you to lead the skunks back here and get them into the shuttle.''

"Lead them back?" Jonathan objected. "They won't obey us. We can't mind-talk at *real* skunks.''

"I've ordered them to follow you two unquestioningly wherever you lead. They're pretty obedient, unless they get hungry. So I've promised them a trove of goodies when they get where they're going. They'll follow. Now, hurry to the clearing. I'm off!''

He rippled off between several startled legs and disappeared into the bushes. Karen and Jonathan looked around them. The crowd nearby had given them a wide berth, but many of the locals had heard about Karen's pet skunk, so the panic was muted.

With sheepish grins, the two slipped away from the staring eyes, then turned and ran furiously for the woods. As they neared the clearing, they slowed down.

"Do you think those skunks are really going to follow us when we get there?" Jonathan asked.

"If not, we're going to be the smelliest kids in three states."

Finally the trees thinned. In the deepening twilight, the ground of the clearing seemed alive, a seething, rippling carpet of black and white.

"Jeeze," Jonathan whispered, "There must be hundreds of them."

At the sound of his voice, everything shifted. A sea of black eyes glinted toward them.

"It's us," Karen said hesitantly. "Remember the ones Stinker said you're to follow? Jonathan, I can't believe I'm actually trying to talk to skunks—real skunks!"

"Well, they haven't sprayed us yet. Let's try walking away and see what happens."

Slowly the two backed out of the clearing. With much rustling and random squeals and chirrups, the furry mob began to follow. Turning forward, Karen and Jonathan headed deliberately back toward their homes. Their little army moved with them until the two were in the middle of a steadily flowing black and white tide.

Suddenly they were within sight of the road, the brightly lit shuttle, and the enormous crowd.

"Courage," Karen said weakly after they'd both slowed to a halt. Jonathan squared his shoulders and jammed his glasses back along his sweaty nose. Then he reconsidered, slipped the glasses off, and stuffed them in a pocket. He had a feeling that if the faces around him were an unrecognizable blur, this whole incredible thing might be easier.

As they started forward, he muttered to Karen, "When this is all over, you realize we're going to be questioned by the CIA, FBI, NASA, and a whole bunch we don't even know about."

"At least that will get us out of school for a few days."

"Hmm."

"Maybe they'll take us someplace interesting."

"Like the torture chamber in the Pentagon basement."

"Oh, hush!"

Resolutely they marched on. People began to notice them now. With startled screams they pushed back out of their way. Like a gust of wind, the screaming spread through the crowd, then was followed by a fearful silence. Everyone seemed frozen into inaction, afraid that any sudden move would set off a monumental stench.

Blushing violently but trying to ignore the onlookers, the two children led their troops toward the shuttle. Skunk odor still wafted from the open hatch.

At the foot of the ladder, the two exchanged a few words, and Jonathan resolutely gripped the rungs and began climbing. With difficulty the skunks followed. Karen stayed at the bottom helping the smaller and clumsier animals. They really were not natural climbers. She concentrated fiercely on what she was doing, ignoring the rising chorus of exclamations and protests.

Several officials began moving toward them. The hindmost skunks turned nervously and began twitching their tails over their heads. Hastily the party retreated.

Cameras whirred, incredulous reporters whispered into microphones. One gruff voice was heard saying, "We've got to start shooting those varmits before they . . ."

"Don't you dare!" whispered another. "That'll set them all off."

Above the mumbling, Karen caught her mother's voice but tried to tune it out. "Karen please, what are you? . . . Oh no, Sancho! Stay away from those skunks!"

Alarmed, Karen looked up. But Stinker must have

given Sancho a parting command as well. The spaniel was sitting in front of the crowd, grinning and thumping his tail.

Suddenly another sound floated to her, one that seemed harmless enough—like the distant clatter of wind chimes.

✸ thirteen ✸

GETAWAY

"JONATHAN!" KAREN CRIED, AS SHE REDOUBLED HER EF-
forts to boost skunks up the ladder, but she could see
from Jonathan's pale wide-eyed face peering out from
the hatch, that he had heard as well.

Gradually members of the crowd seemed to hear it
too and began turning curiously toward the woods.
"Great God in Heaven!" someone yelled. "What are
those?"

Heads swiveled, voices screamed—screamed in abso-
lute horror this time. People began pushing back from
the fringe of trees. From out of the woods strode a
cluster of poles held at the top by a pulsing gelatinous
mass. Several other creatures clattered after it.

The things marched forward knocking down and step-
ping on panicky people in their path. A few soldiers and

police hurriedly raised their guns and fired but with no noticeable effect. As if swatting flies, several Zarnk raised metal-tipped pole-arms, and a line of trucks in the army barricade vanished in an orange glow. Pandemonium.

"Look," Jonathan yelled from his vantage point, "one of them's carrying sort of a clear box. There's something black and white inside."

"They've captured Stinker!" Karen's cry could scarcely be heard over the chaos of gunshots and cries of the crowd.

"They're coming this way! Maybe they're after the shuttle, too. We've got to stop them!"

"We've got to save Stinker!"

Now a dozen of the creatures had cleared the woods. As people scrambled out of their way and soldiers fired at them, the aliens continued stalking toward the shuttle. The ship that had earlier looked so awesome and exciting suddenly seemed cold and alone in the white glare of abandoned TV lights.

Karen looked down at the small skunk kitten nuzzling in her arms. She'd been helping it up the ladder when the Zarnk appeared. Thoughtfully she put the little animal back on the ground. "Jonathan, what about the secret weapon?"

"Huh? Skunk spray? But *we* can't think at them to go spray the Zarnk. And Stinker's cage must be thought-proof, or he would have tried by now."

"I guess so. But . . . no, wait. He's *already* ordered

them to follow us. All we have to do is lead the attack. Let's go!''

Jonathan stared aghast as Karen hopped over the skunks around her and ran down the road toward the advancing Zarnk. He glanced behind him at the agitated mass of black and white. "Okay guys, follow us!" He scrambled down the ladder. "Charge!"

With little grace but great vigor, skunks poured out of the ship and joined those still on the ground in pelting after the two children. At first the Zarnk ignored them—the little animals hardly looked threatening—but as the strange army drew closer, the lead Zarnk raised one of its poles. It pointed the glinting metallic tip at the leaders.

Karen and Jonathan, running abreast, skidded to a halt. In wide-eyed horror they looked at each other, then threw themselves to the asphalt. Confused, the skunks milled about. Suddenly leaderless, they were left to nothing but their instincts.

As the threatening Zarnk advanced, scores of skunks spun around. Here, clearly, was an enemy. Nearly in unison they raised their tails and shot an oily cloud of stench.

Startled silence fell on the fleeing humans and Zarnk alike. Then high piercing wails split the air. The tall Zarnk began staggering blindly about. Their tops whitened and flaked away, leaving their legs to fall like dry bones to the surface of the road.

A clear box fell from the grip of one and cracked

open as it bounced over the asphalt. Dizzily, a black and white creature stumbled out.

The two children lay curled up on the road like sow bugs, but nothing could keep out the awful burning stench. Coughing, eyes clenched shut against the stinging spray, Karen wondered if it might not have been better to be zapped by a Zarnk ray gun.

"Nonsense," said a familiar voice in her mind. She felt a soft furry muzzle push against her face. Opening her tear-streaming eyes, she looked into a pair of black beady ones.

"Thanks, guys. That was some rescue. Those jerks thought I was one of this planet's big shots and were holding me hostage in exchange for the Sylon spy they thought was hiding here. Good thing they don't pick up minds too well. I don't know what they thought you humans were—wildlife maybe. But that ship must have looked just too good to leave alone."

"Oh, Stinker!" Karen said, barely able to talk for the gagging stench in the air. She picked the little creature up and hugged him.

Jonathan looked about, trying to ignore the withering bits of Zarnk. Those people who had not run completely away were standing at a distance, coughing and fanning their hands in the air, but a few soldiers were beginning to stumble back their way.

"We'd better get the little general and his army back to the shuttle. Skunks may stink, but they're not as permanently off-putting as those Zarnk guys."

"Stink?" Stinker thought indignantly. "I'll have you know . . ."

"No, you won't," Karen said as, holding him tight, she scrambled to her feet and ran back up the road. "It's daring getaway time."

Under orders once more, the victorious skunks dutifully padded after the children. Soon they were again clambering into the shuttle. This time Stinker stood at the top directing operations while Karen and Jonathan both boosted skunks up the ladder.

The man with the medals was weaving his way toward them, a handkerchief to his nose. "See here, those creatures must get out of there. That's government property!"

"It's okay, sir," Jonathan shouted. "They're American skunks—most of them."

"If you kids don't stop that and tell us what on earth is going on . . ." The man broke into a coughing fit and retreated as a new cloud of stench sailed his way.

"Time to go," Stinker said, lowering his tail. "Thanks for everything. You've been real friends, you know. Now, keep it up with each other if you can."

"Sure," Jonathan replied with a blush. The last little skunk left his hands and pulled itself up the ladder.

Karen looked up at the plump leader, incongruously majestic at the edge of the hatch. "Stinker, we'll miss you."

"Hey, don't be sad. This is a pretty fair planet, you know. I'll put in a glowing report when I get home. Maybe they'll set up trade relations or something."

"We can ship you tons of peanut butter," Karen said, trying to smile.

"Right! And in any case, I'll try and drop by here. You two ought to go on a *real* space adventure sometime. You're just the type for it. Oops, got to go."

A troop of soldiers was trotting their way, rifles in hand. Stinker dropped from sight and the hatch closed. Jonathan pulled away the ladder. "Got to get this back to my dad," he shouted as he and Karen ran off.

A few soldiers halfheartedly headed after them, then turned back and joined the others who were milling about the shuttle and banging on anything they could reach.

The bemedaled man, his uniform reeking of skunk, was stamping about, shouting, "How could those little beasts possibly close the door? How on earth are we going to get them out of there? What were . . ."

Suddenly the ship shuddered. A rumble began deep within and built to a roar as the engine burst into life.

"It can't do that!" the man yelled hysterically as he and the others ran back from the noise and heat. "It can't start up like that!"

A reporter popped out of a bush where he'd been cowering with his cameraman. "Sir," he said, thrusting a microphone into the frazzled man's face, "can it take off from here?" He had to yell above the engine noise.

"Of course not, idiot! No booster rockets. It's not powered for it. And anyway, there's just a bunch of skunks in there, for crying out loud!"

White heat glowed from the engines, and slowly the

shuttle moved forward. Purple with rage, the army man just stared and pointed. It rolled into the Waldrons' barnyard, turned around, and headed back up the road, gathering speed as it went.

An army roadblock of trucks stretched across the road ahead. The soldiers still manning the trucks leaped into the beanfields as the roaring spacecraft bore down upon them.

With a sudden burst of power, the shuttle's nose jerked upward, and the ship rose at an officially impossible angle into the sky.

From the Waldrons' front porch, Karen and Jonathan watched as it climbed into the night, a great white stripe against a field of soft black.

To Karen it looked familiar. "I wonder why no one ever named a constellation 'The Skunk?' "

"Maybe on another planet someone has," Jonathan suggested, "or will."

"And maybe we'll get a chance to find out someday."

The two friends looked at each other and grinned.

About the Author

PAMELA F. SERVICE, a native of Berkeley, California, now lives in Bloomington, Indiana. She is a graduate of the University of California at Berkeley and holds a master's degree from the University of London. Ms. Service is a museum curator and a member of Bloomington's City Council. Among her previously published novels are *Winter of Magic's Return*, *A Question of Destiny*, *When the Night Wind Howls*, and *Tomorrow's Magic*.